This book is dedicated to
my three children Mykal, Jacqui, and Carter
- the best kids anyone could ever ask for.

Created by Vince Daubenspeck
Waialua, Hawai‘i 96791

www.humptydumptybooks.com

Designed and Distributed by

ISLAND HERITAGE™
A DIVISION OF THE MADDEN CORPORATION

ISBN:1-61710-195-8
First Edition, Third Printing—2014

COP 141405

KOHOLĀ
King of the Whales

By Vince Daubenspeck

Illustrated by Don Robinson

Kekela and the old man wandered on the lava point, two colorful shapes against the bright blue sky. They were exploring the little tide pools, looking at the life held captive. Minnows darted into holes as little hermit crabs scurried around. Grandpa followed Kekela, hopping from hole to hole, answering as many questions as he could.

Suddenly, Kekela stopped and pointed toward a giant splash out in the ocean. "Grandpa, why do whales jump up in the air like that?" Kekela had a puzzled look on his face as he looked out across the waves.

Grandpa stretched his hand out to the ocean as he answered. "Kekela, that is a wonderful story from a very long time ago. Come over here and have a seat with me." Grandpa gathered his little boy in his lap and began the story his Grandmother had told him a lifetime ago:

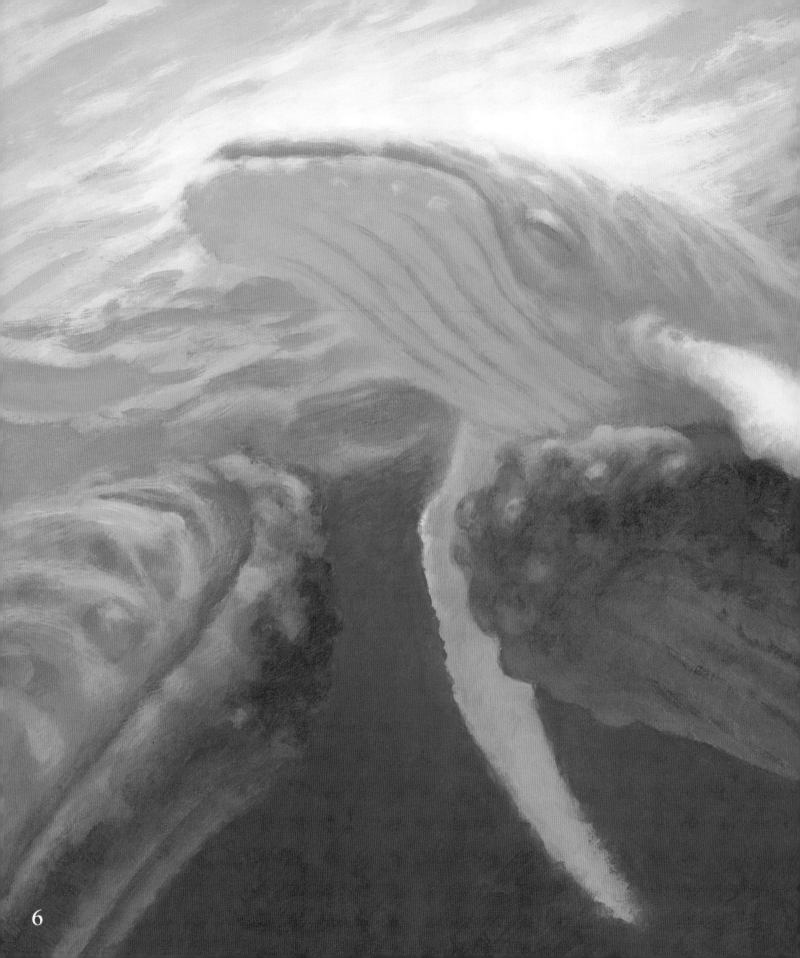

A long, long time ago, a mother and father whale came to our islands here in the middle of the Pacific Ocean. The loving pair had traveled from the north as whales had done for ages, swimming to our warm, safe waters to give birth. It was a peaceful time and the exciting day finally came. Mother was filled with joy as she nudged her new baby to the surface for his first breath of air. Father proudly looked over his newborn and examined his bright eyes, strong tail, and extra long pectoral fins. He could barely hold back his excitement just wondering what a fine whale his son would become. Mother and Father decided to name him Koholā, after some of their great ancestors.

The whale family passed the days resting in the warm blue waters. Floating lazily along, Mother and Father met many other whale couples with young ones. Father could not help but compare his little boy, with his extra long fins, to the other new arrivals. Koholā grew fast and strong and Father was extremely proud. The other adult whales also noticed how strong Koholā was becoming, but the young whales laughed at his long, clumsy fins. Koholā felt very awkward and wished his fins were shorter, like everyone else's. Sadly, he started to spend a lot of time alone, exploring the wide blue sea.

The time soon came to leave the warm Hawaiian waters and head back to the northern seas. Koholā grew faster and stronger every day and all of the other whales were amazed by his daring antics. Much to his mother's dismay, he swam deeper than any of the other young whales and he loved to sneak up on the grown-ups, scaring them as he raced by as fast as he could. His extra long fins seemed to propel him with special power and speed through the beautiful, sparkling sea.

One day, Koholā told his mother he was going to go down deep into the dark part of the ocean, turn around, and swim as fast as he could toward the bright spot above the water. "You'll do no such thing!" cried Mother. "It's dangerous above the water. We are forbidden to go there." She gave Father a concerned look, but Father didn't know what to say.

From then on, whenever Koholā went up for a breath, he did his best to lean to one side and look above the water. Whether he saw the dark of night, flashing storm clouds, or clear shining light, the open sky above never seemed dangerous to him. One day, he couldn't resist any longer. Koholā decided to poke his head up so that both of his eyes were above the water at the same time.

He went off by himself, dove down, turned his huge body, and gave
a few pushes with his extra long fins.

He broke through the top of the water with a sudden lightness and came crashing back through the waves. It was very scary.

Koholā caught his breath and took a few moments to figure out what had just happened. He had gone above the water. And nothing bad had happened. Not yet, anyway.

As Grandpa waved his hands and told the story, Kekela laughed, spread his arms, and jumped in the air like Koholā.

Over the next few days, while the other young whales played together, Koholā went off on his own to work on his new skill. He explored the ocean depths and the forbidden place above the water. He dove even deeper, pushed even harder with his extra long fins, and went even higher into the air. He felt more and more of the lightness and it gave him such a feeling of freedom and energy! And he did his best to make sure no one found out about his adventures.

19

One day, Kohola was off by himself practicing his leaps. On his way down to the darker depths, he noticed something new out of the corner of his eye. He took a better look and saw it was one of the bad dark-light enemies Mother had warned him about. He could hear her voice in the back of his mind telling him that whales always swam together to protect against the dark-lights. He turned away and saw another dark-light...and another...and another. He was surrounded!

Waves of fear started at the tips of his fins, shot up his back, and crashed into his brain. He had to get away! Turning toward the light, he flipped his tail harder than he had ever done before and pushed his extra long fins with all his might. With his heart pounding, he reached the top of the water and closed his eyes for what he thought might be the last time.

It seemed like the lightness lasted forever. He opened his eyes and the pounding of his heart stopped. The top of the water glittered as it passed below him and he took a deeper breath than he could imagine possible. As he finally dropped down to the top of the water, it all became clear. It was clear he had left the dark-lights way behind him, and now it was crystal clear to Koholā where he fit with his own kind and the other creatures in the ocean.

As Koholā grew in skill and strength, he also grew in wisdom, well beyond any of the others. Not only could he escape the danger to himself; he also became an expert at coming to the aid of his family and friends.

He could crash through the top of the water with great power and scare away the dark-lights and any other threats that might be around. Because of the selfless way he helped all those around him, the whales loved and respected him and called him Koholā, King of the Whales.

Koholā tried to teach all the other whales everything he had learned, but none of the other whales had his strength, his courage, or his extra long fins. Year after year, the whales made trip after trip from the cold northern seas to the beautiful warm Hawaiian waters. Koholā continued to teach his kind, but none of the others ever became as wise or skillful as he had become.

Finally, after a lifetime of protecting others, the time came for Koholā to be with his ancestors. He was greatly missed by all, but his legend has never been forgotten. All whales look forward to the day when a new King of the Whales will be born. They know he will have extra long fins and be able to glide over the ocean waves. So far, though, no whale but Koholā has been able to soar above the water.

But, to this day, you can see them trying the best they can...

Grandpa took an extra long breath when he finished his tale. Kekela leaned back and relaxed in his Grandpa's loving lap. They sat quietly at the edge of the ocean for the rest of the evening and watched for a whale...with extra long fins.

Dive deep and jump for the stars...